For Paul Lawrence Hackett
with love

A catalogue record for this book is available from the British Library
Published by Ladybird Books Ltd Loughborough Leicestershire UK
Ladybird Books Ltd is a subsidiary of the Penguin Group of companies

by Judith Nicholls
illustrated by Robin Davies

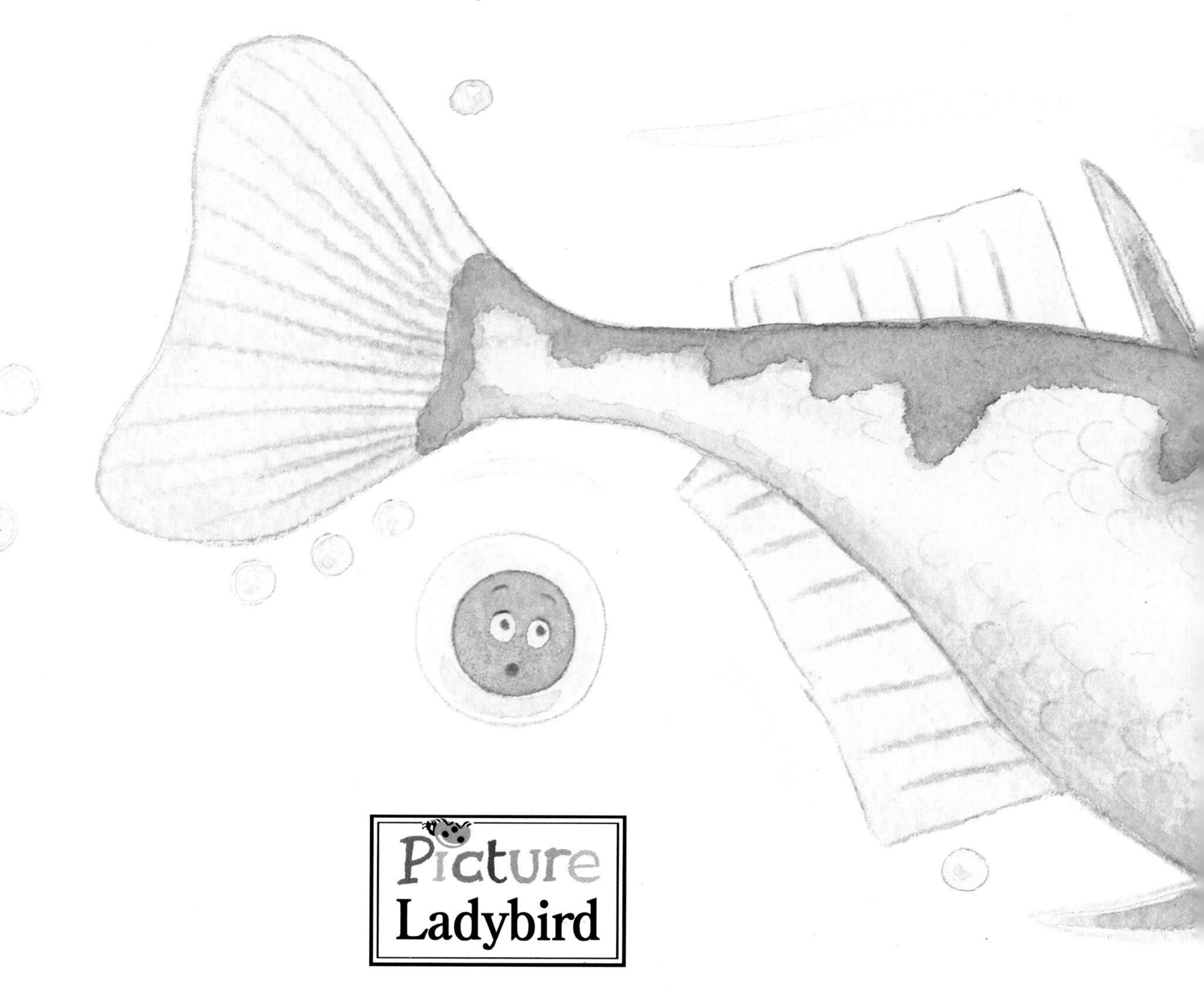

Picture
Ladybird

George was sad.

He couldn't jump, he couldn't jiggle.

He couldn't run, he couldn't wriggle.

All he could do was…

dream,

drifting by the weeds

in the dark, dark pond.

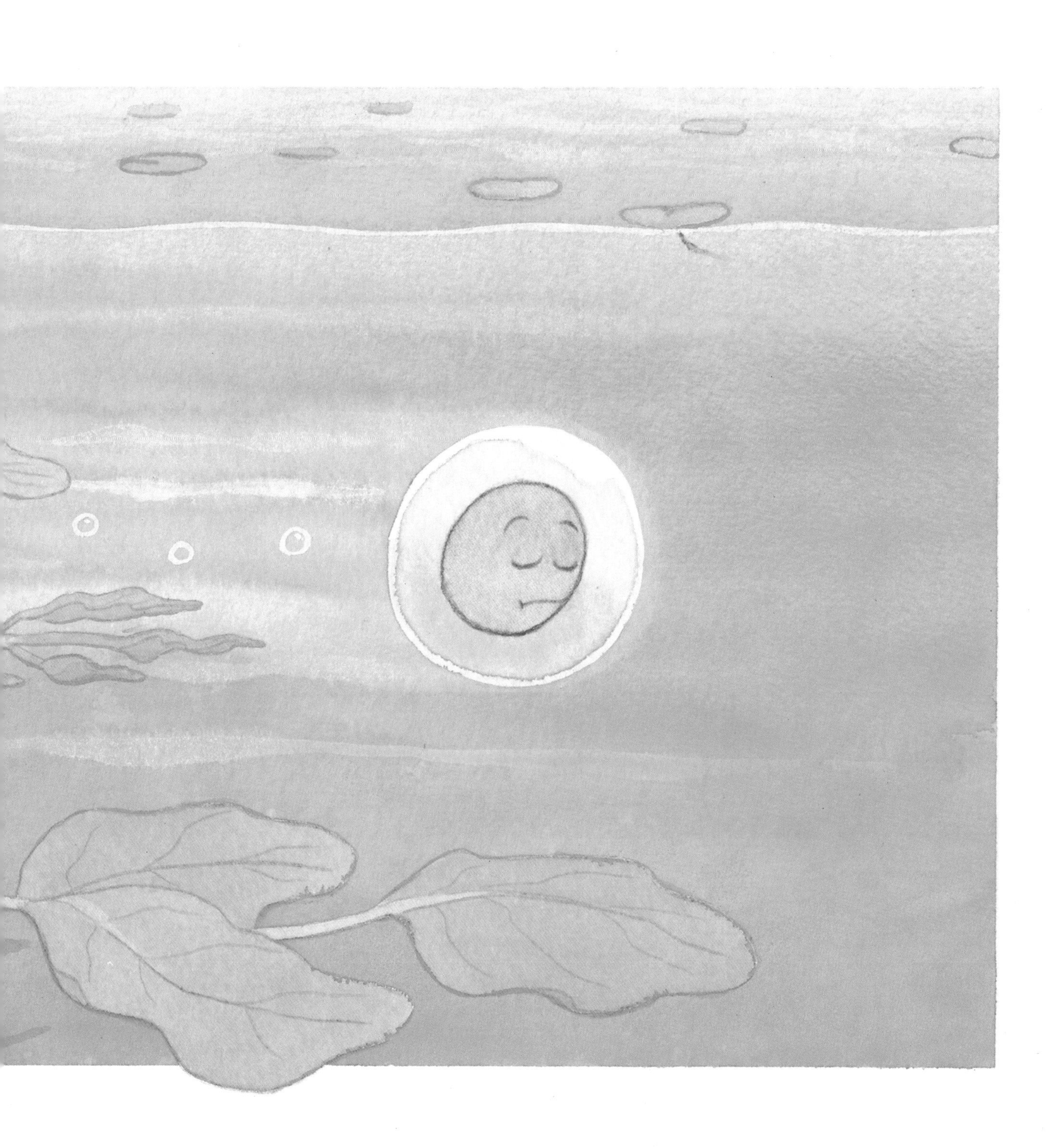

"Who am I?" he asked the water-boatman.

The water-boatman was far too busy to stop.

He stared crossly.

"Who are you?
You're a dot,
you're a spot,
you're a jelly-belly tot.
You're an inky-pinky blot
in the dark, dark pond!"

The water-boatman kicked his legs proudly,
and darted away through
the weedy water.

George was sad.

He couldn't dart,
he couldn't hop.
He couldn't start,
he couldn't stop.

All he could do was dream,
drifting by the weeds
in the dark, dark pond.

"Who am I?"
he asked the stickleback.
The stickleback wriggled closer,
then she giggled.

"Who are you?
You're a dot,
you're a spot,
you're a jelly-belly tot.
You're an inky-pinky blot
in the dark, dark pond!"

The stickleback flicked her tail proudly,
and danced away through
the weedy water.

George waited sadly.
He couldn't dance,
he couldn't kick.
He couldn't glide,
he couldn't flick.

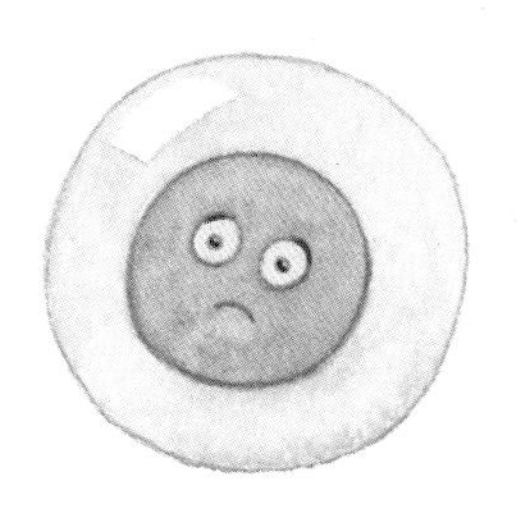

But each day he grew just
a little bigger...

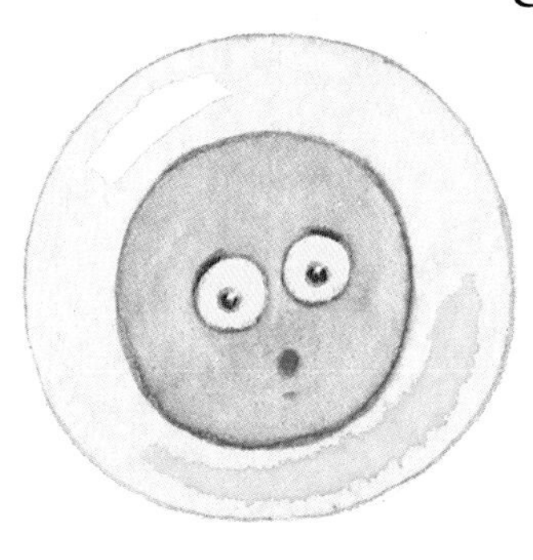

and bigger...

and bigger...

One day the stickleback wriggled past again.

"Fiddle-my-fins,
Fiddle-my-fins –
you're getting fat!
And fiddle-my-
fiddledy-diddledy-fins –
just what do you think
is THAT?"

George looked behind

to find a...

TAIL!

He waved it, he wiggled it.

He flicked it, he jiggled it.

"Now who am I?" he asked in excitement.

"Pooh! I've already told you that,"

said the stickleback, rudely.

"You're a dot,
you're a spot,
you're a jelly-belly tot.
You're an inky-pinky blot
in the dark, dark pond!"

"I'm NOT!" cried George.
"I'm not, I'm not, I'm *NOT*!"

And this time,
to his surprise,
he darted forward.
The stickleback
wriggled off in alarm.

Each day George grew bigger…

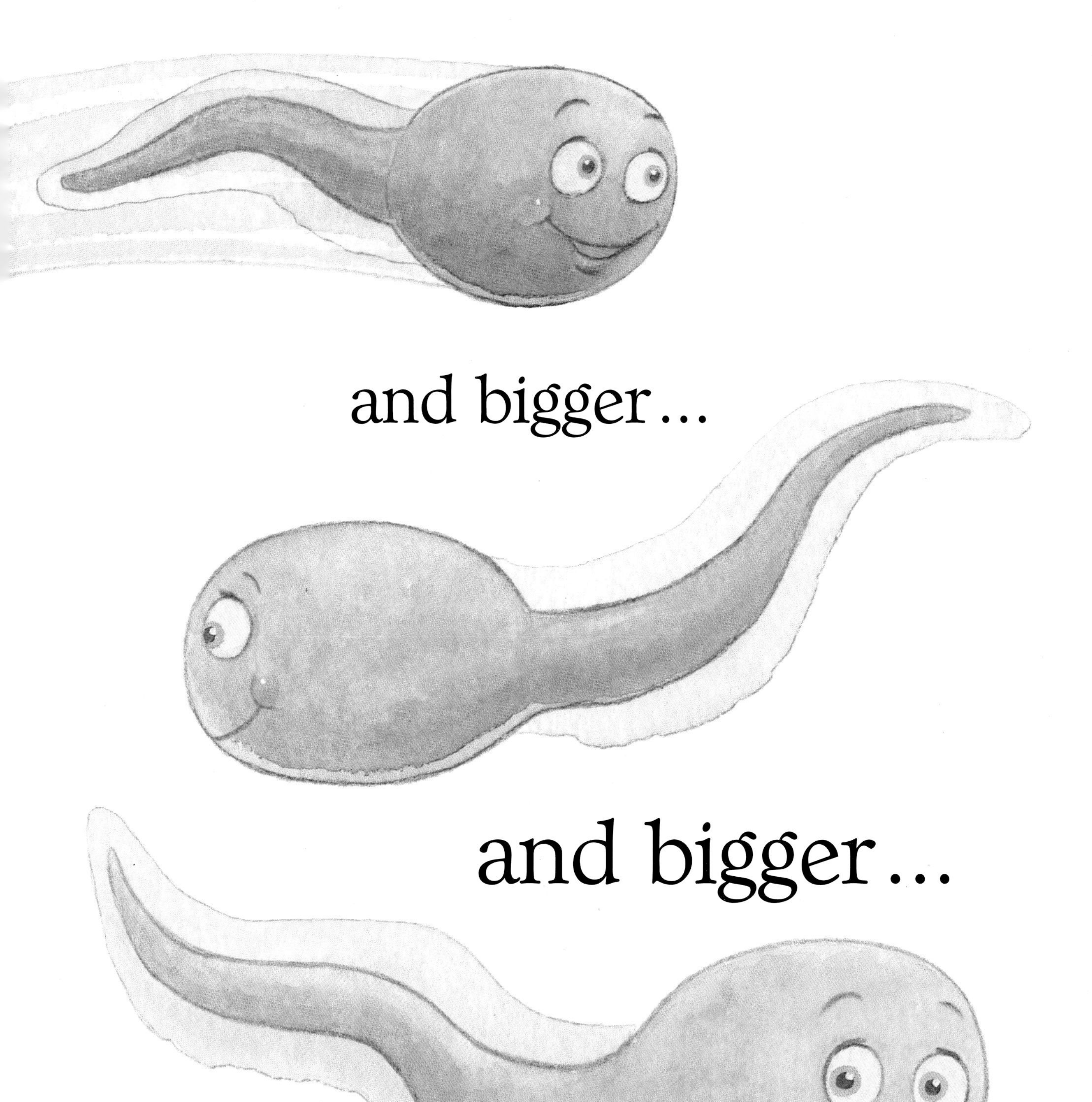

and bigger…

and bigger…

One day the water-boatman darted by again.
When he saw George this time
he stopped and stared.
He looked puzzled.

"What's this?
You're not a dot
or a spot!
You're not a jelly-belly tot
any longer."

George looked behind
to find...

LEGS!

He looked, he kicked,
he licked his lips.

The water-boatman darted off in alarm,
and George kicked again.

He landed rather breathlessly
on a slithery, sunny rock by the edge
of the dark, dark pond.
He stared around. Then he smiled
and blinked happily.

"I can do it!"

"I can dance, I can kick,
I can glide, I can flick!

I can jump, I can jiggle,
I can race, I can wriggle!

I can swim, I can hop,
I can jelly-belly flop!

I can leap to a leaf,
I can dive to a log!

I can slide, I can hide,
I am ME!   I am…

FROG!"